USBORNE FIRST
Level

The Ugly Duckling

Based on the story
by Hans Christian Andersen

Retold by Fiona Patchett
Illustrated by Valentina Fontana

Reading consultant: Alison Kelly

Once there was a Mother
Duck who lived by a lake.

She sat on her nest keeping
her eggs warm.

But she waited...

...and waited...

...and waited.

Finally, she got up and
looked at the eggs.
One,
two,
three,
four,
five...

...smooth, white eggs. The
sixth egg was huge – and blue!

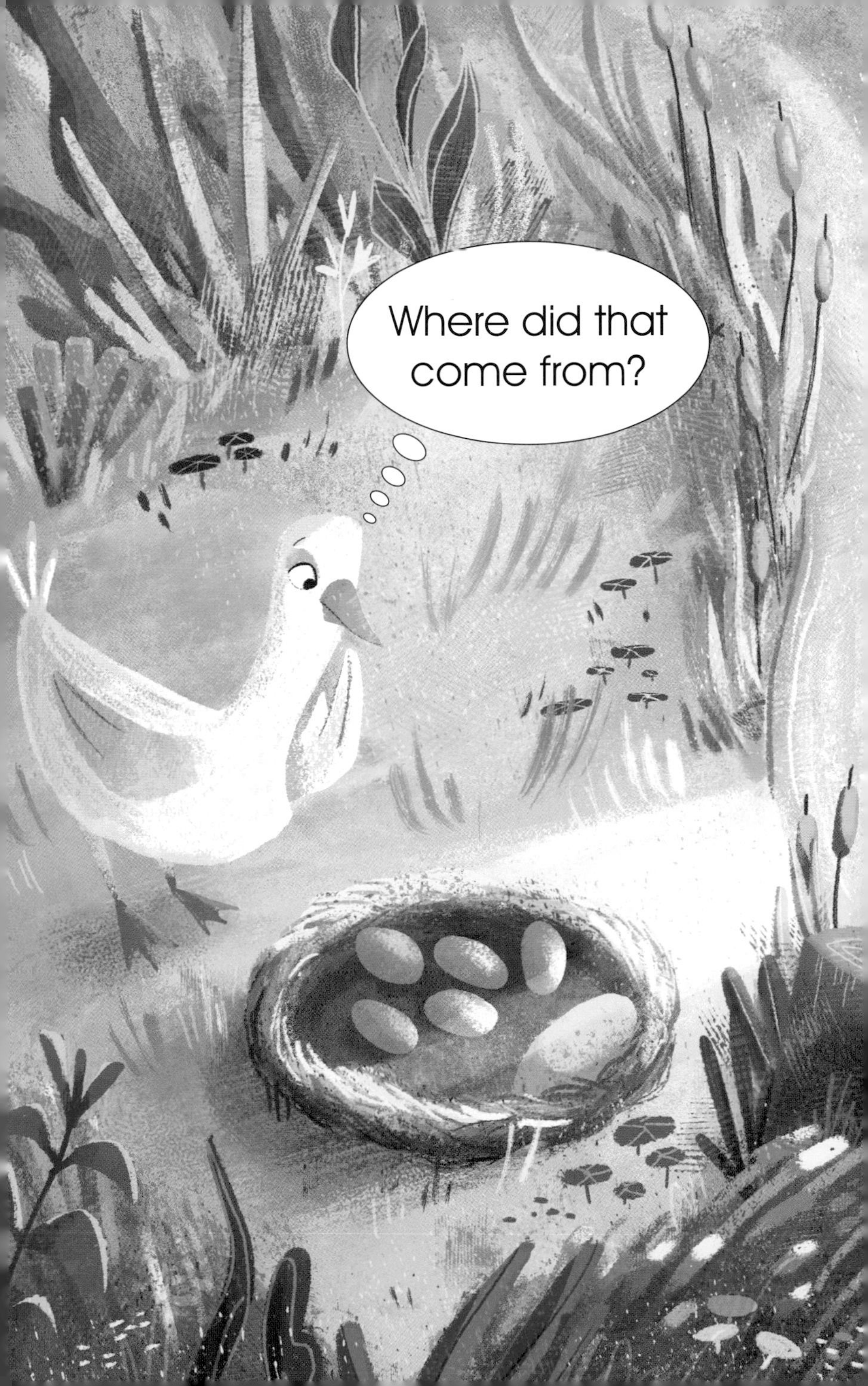
Where did that come from?

She heard a tap-tap-tap...

CRACK!

A fluffy, yellow duckling popped out of one egg.

Then another...

...and another.

Soon five fluffy, yellow
ducklings were running about.

Mother Duck was delighted.

"Come and see my ducklings," she called to her friends.

"Look! I have one, two, three, four, five..."

Oh!

The huge egg was still there.

13

"That's a turkey's egg," said
Old Duck. "Take my advice
and leave it alone."

Just then, there was
a giant...

CRACK!

A beak appeared and there
was a big, scruffy chick.

Mother Duck, her friends
and the ducklings stared.

"He's enormous! He must be a turkey," said one duck.

"We'll find out," said Old Duck. "See if he can swim."

18

The fluffy, yellow ducklings
jumped into the lake.

Splish!

Splash!

Splosh!

The scruffy chick jumped
in too...

Splash!

...and he swam as well as
a duckling!

"Oh," said Old Duck.
"He must just be a very
ugly duckling!"

The fluffy, yellow ducklings played in the water.

When the Ugly Duckling
tried to join them, they
swam away.

Why won't
they play with
me?

Mother Duck felt sad to see
the Ugly Duckling alone.

But the fluffy ducklings
still ignored him.

"There must be other chicks like me," he thought.

"I'm going to find them."

He crossed some fields and came to a farmyard.

May I play with you?

The hens and turkeys took
one look at him and laughed.

The farm girl turned in
surprise. "What's all this
fuss?" she said.

"Where did you come from?" she asked the duckling. "Shoo! Shoo!"

You don't belong here.

The little duckling ran until
he reached a bush. Two birds
glared at him.

"Where did you come
from?" they squawked.
"Leave us alone!"

29

Tired and lonely, the Ugly
Duckling went to sleep
beside a pond.

In the morning, he was
woken up by some wild geese.

Then...

...two men appeared.

The wild geese flew away
as fast as they could.

Some dogs came splashing
through the pond.

One dog barked at the
Ugly Duckling.

Then he growled and ran off.

An icy wind began to blow.
The duckling saw a house. It
looked so warm, he crept in.

"May I stay here for the
night?" he asked.

"Of course," said the old lady. "I hope you lay eggs."

The Ugly Duckling settled
in and stayed over the winter.
By spring, he had grown.

"I'm afraid you'll have to go," said the old lady. "I can't afford to keep you."

The duckling flew for
weeks. At last, he came to
a lake with three swans.

He hid behind some reeds,
so they couldn't see him.

One swan saw the Ugly
Duckling and glided over.

"You have the whitest
feathers I have ever seen!"
said the swan.

"Don't make fun of me," said the duckling. "I know I'm ugly."

"Ugly? Look in the water!"
said the swan.

The Ugly Duckling bent his
neck and saw...

...he was no longer an
ugly duckling, but a
beautiful swan.

He lived happily with his new friends. One day, some children came to the lake.

"Look at the new swan," they said. "He is the most beautiful of them all!"

About the story

The Ugly Duckling was first told by Hans Christian Andersen, who was born in Denmark in 1805. When he was young he was shy and awkward, but he grew up to be famous all over the world for his wonderful fairy tales.

Designed by Sam Whibley
Series designer: Russell Punter
Series editor: Lesley Sims

First published in 2020 by Usborne Publishing Ltd.,
Usborne House, 83-85 Saffron Hill, London EC1N 8RT, England.
usborne.com Copyright © 2020 Usborne Publishing Ltd.

USBORNE FIRST READING
Level Four